Palapalooza

by Daphne Skinner
illustrated by Jerry Smath

Kane Press, Inc.
New York

To Samantha and Katlyn Maguire—J.S.

Library of Congress Cataloging-in-Publication Data

Skinner, Daphne.
    Palapalooza / by Daphne Skinner ; illustrated by Jerry Smath.
        p. cm. — (Social·studies connects)
    "Culture/Holidays - Grades: K-2."
    Summary: Bored after the end of winter holidays, Carter and George
and their friends create a new holiday to celebrate.
    ISBN 1-57565-163-7 (alk. paper)
    [1. Friendship—Fiction. 2. Holidays—Fiction.]   I. Smath, Jerry, ill.
II. Title. III. Series.
PZ7.S6277Pal 2006
[E]—dc22
                                        2005018679

10 9 8 7 6 5 4 3 2 1

First published in the United States of America in 2006 by Kane Press, Inc.
Printed in Hong Kong.

Book Design: Edward Miller

Social Studies Connects is a trademark of Kane Press, Inc.

www.kanepress.com

"January is so boring," Carter complained. "All the best holidays are over. New Year's, Christmas, Hanukkah, Kwanzaa—gone!"

"There's always next year," said his brother, George.

Carter did a trick on his skateboard. "A year is *forever*," he groaned.

Their friends felt the same way.

"Too bad the Fourth of July doesn't come in January," said Meg.

"Or Halloween," added Carter.

"Remember carving that giant pumpkin?" Eva asked.

"And eating pumpkin pie!" said Denzel.

"*Mmm*," George said. "Now, that's a holiday!"

Holidays are days on which we celebrate or remember things that are important to us.

A jack-o'-lantern is a **symbol** of Halloween. Other holidays have symbols, too.

5

Denzel pulled out his pocket calendar. "All is not lost," he said. "Presidents' Day is coming up, and Martin Luther King Day. Not to mention Brain Awareness Day!"

"Brain Day?" asked Meg. "No offense, Denzel, but I think we need a holiday that's *fun*."

Lots of holidays—like Presidents' Day and Martin Luther King Jr. Day—honor leaders and heroes. The British celebrate the Queen's Birthday. In Japan they celebrate the Emperor's Birthday.

"The kind with presents," Carter chimed in.
"And costumes," said Eva.
"And meals with cool desserts," added George.
The friends looked at each other and sighed.

"What if we made up a holiday?" Eva asked.

"We could," said Denzel. "But I still like Brain
Awareness Day."
George grinned. "You would," he said.

"What about *Pet* Awareness Day?" Meg
suggested. "We could have presents, and costumes,
and food—and our pets could play together!"
"Fun!" said Eva.
They decided to try it.

People do special things on
holidays, like giving presents or
coloring eggs or watching parades.

At first it was fun.
The pets wore costumes.
They ate pet treats.
Some did tricks—
and some didn't.

One American holiday—Groundhog Day—stars an animal! If a groundhog sees his shadow on February 2, we say spring will come in six weeks.

Spring is celebrated in different ways all over the world. The Japanese have a cherry blossom festival. In Pakistan people fly kites—thousands of them!

TURTLE TRICKS

11

Then Eva tried to take a group photo.
That didn't go so well.

The next day everybody was glum.

"We need a new holiday idea," George said.

"But no pets," said Meg. "Perky is still recovering."

Denzel was leafing through a giant book. "Look at all these washing and cleaning holidays."

"Yuck! I'd be happy if I never washed again," said Carter. "My dream holiday wouldn't even allow soap!"

In many countries, homes are cleaned from top to bottom to celebrate the New Year.

HOLIDAYS OF THE WORLD

"I love sloppy days," said Meg. "Why don't we have a sloppy holiday? We could sleep until noon—"

"And wear yesterday's clothes," added Carter.

"And eat with our hands," said Eva.

"And have a food fight at lunch!" yelled George.

"A slobfest!" Carter said. "Brilliant!"

Slobfest ended before it began.
Nobody was allowed to sleep until noon.
Or wear dirty clothes.
Or eat with their hands.
"My mother screamed when she saw me," said
Carter. "I had to take a shower *and* wash my hair!"

"My mom said I could wear dirty clothes if I cleaned out my closet. So I told her I'd wear *clean* clothes," Eva complained. "But she made me clean out the closet anyway!"

"That is *so* unfair!" said Meg.

"Let's just think of something else," Denzel suggested. "Something less gross."

"How about a Chocolate Fest?" asked George.

Everybody loved the idea.

On Saturday they had an all-chocolate jamboree. Everyone gobbled up George's home-baked brownies. They drank chocolate milk and hot cocoa. They made hot fudge sundaes with chocolate ice cream and jumbo chocolate Gummi bears.

Food holidays are popular all over the world. Some African countries have yam festivals, and in parts of Asia there are rice festivals. On Bun Day in Iceland, everybody eats cream puffs!

19

They all got terrible stomachaches.
Then things got even worse.

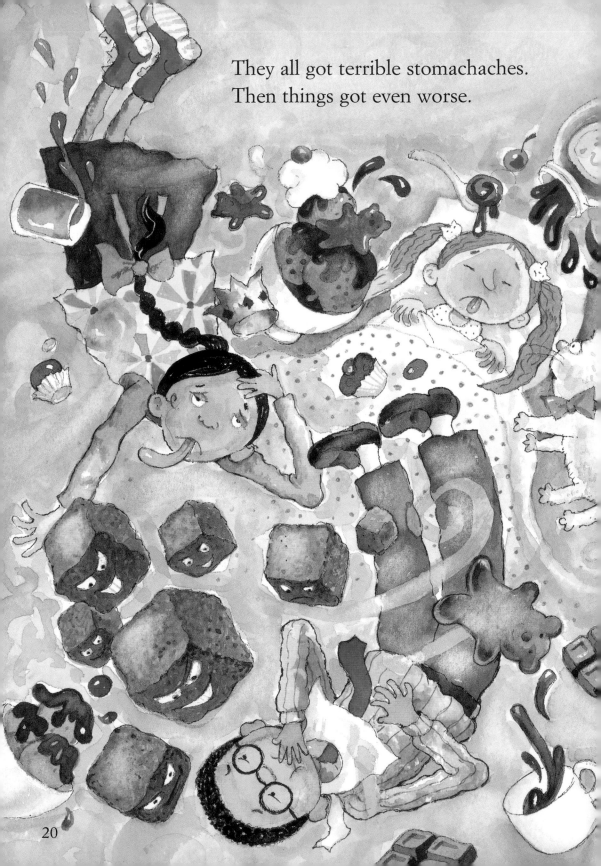

That night, Carter and George found out that they were moving.

They called their friends and gave them the bad news. Everybody felt sad.

Just before bedtime, Denzel took out his journal and wrote.

He wrote about being friends with Carter and George.

He wrote about how much he'd miss them.

BRAIN BLASTER CHAMP

PIZZA

CARTER & GEORGE

Junior Champ CARTER

CONGRATULATIONS DENZEL!

From George and Carter

Meg told Perky about Carter and George. "I know they're only moving three towns away, but it's not even in the same area code."

"Cheer up!" squawked Perky. But Meg couldn't.

Eva stayed up late trying to think of a going-away present for her friends. She got a great idea right before she fell asleep.

"I was thinking about you guys," Eva said the next day. "And I figured out the perfect holiday!"

"Moving Day?" muttered George.

"No," replied Eva, "Friendship Day!"

"A holiday in honor of being friends?" Denzel perked up. "That *is* perfect!"

"We could call it Palapalooza!" Meg yelled.

Some holidays—like Mother's Day and Father's Day—are about the people who are important to us.

Palapalooza was sunny and warm.
The kids met in the park with their skateboards,
and Carter taught them how to do tricks.

Sports and games are part of lots of holidays. China's Dragon Boat Festival features boat races. During Dano, a Korean holiday, men have wrestling matches and women swing on swings.

They skated over to Denzel's house to play Brain Blaster. He won, as usual.

Next they went to Meg's house and watched *A Wolf Named Cuddles* and *Revenge of the Kittens*.

When it was time for supper they went to George and Carter's house.

Eva put up decorations.

They ate their favorite foods—pizza, and George's famous triple-layer chocolate cake.

PALAPALOOZA

Some holidays are celebrated by millions of people. Others are celebrated by just a few.

They exchanged presents.
They posed for a group photo.

When it was time to go home, nobody wanted to leave.

"We should do this again," said Eva.

"It's a perfect holiday," George pointed out. "Games, food, presents . . ."

"And a celebration of something really special—good friends," Denzel added.

"Let's make Palapalooza a tradition," Meg chimed in. "And celebrate it every year!"

So they did.
And January was never boring again.

Every single day is a holiday somewhere in the world.

We understand traditions!

So do we!

MAKING CONNECTIONS

Traditions are things you do every time a holiday comes around, like planting a tree on Arbor Day, or making a piñata on Cinco de Mayo, or wearing green on St. Patrick's Day. Do you watch fireworks on the Fourth of July? That's a tradition you share with lots of Americans. Traditions are often passed down through many generations. What traditions does your family have?

Look Back

- Read page 9. What traditions does Meg want to include in Pet Awareness Day?
- On page 14, what holiday tradition gives the kids the idea for Slobfest?
- Look at page 24. What is Palapalooza in honor of?
- On pages 25–27, what traditions of their own do the friends celebrate?
- Turn to pages 30–31. Does Palapalooza become a tradition?

Try This!

Invent your own holiday!
Make a list of your favorite traditions from the holidays that you and your family celebrate. Then invent a new holiday. Choose traditions from your list that fit best with the kind of holiday you are creating. For example, what traditions would help you celebrate a Family Day—or your very own Friendship Day?

Favorite Traditions
1. Carving pumpkins
2. Grandma's homemade gingerbread
3. Wrapping gifts